This
Big Golden Book®
belongs to

randomhousekids.com
ISBN 978-0-7364-3384-6
Printed in the United States of America
10 9 8 7 6 5 4 3 2 1

![Disney]
ZOOTOPIA

Adapted by
BILL SCOLLON

Illustrated by
THE DISNEY STORYBOOK ART TEAM

A GOLDEN BOOK • NEW YORK

ZOOTOPIA WAS A MODERN METROPOLIS where all mammals lived together happily, whether large, small, or anywhere in between.

The city even had neighborhoods to make residents feel comfortable—including Tundratown, Sahara Square, and the Rainforest District.

Out in rural Bunnyburrow, little Judy Hopps was performing in the Carrot Days play. She loved that predators and prey had evolved to live together in harmony. In Zootopia, anyone could be anything!

Later, after the play was over, Judy heard a fox snarling. He was a kid from school, trying to bully some of her friends.

"Gimme your tickets, you meek little sheep!"

Judy boldly stepped in to help—and she got the tickets back! She already knew she wanted to be a police officer when she grew up.

Years later, her dream came true! Judy became the first bunny to join the Zootopia Police Department.

When she headed out for her first real job in the city, Judy's parents were proud of her, but they still didn't fully trust predators.

"Especially foxes," said her dad. He gave Judy a can of fox repellent to take with her, just in case.

Chief Bogo doubted that Judy could make it as a cop. He believed police work was for big, strong animals, not bunnies.

There were fourteen missing mammal cases, but Bogo assigned those investigations to other officers.

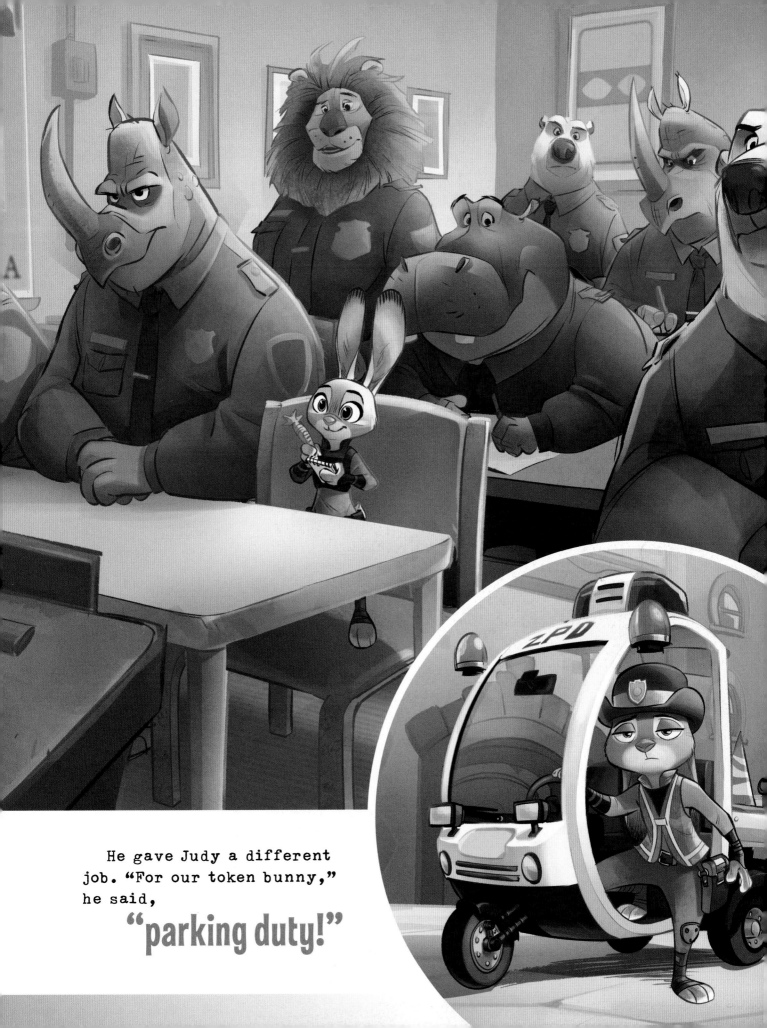

He gave Judy a different job. "For our token bunny," he said, **"parking duty!"**

Judy was disappointed. She wanted to solve real crimes. Still, she was determined to prove she was capable.

Using all her bunny skills, especially her excellent bunny hearing, she wrote 200 parking tickets by lunchtime!

Then Judy noticed a suspicious-looking fox. He was acting strange, so she followed him into a nearby café.

FREQUENT STOPS

To Judy's surprise, the fox was not a criminal.
His name was Nick Wilde and he was just trying to order
a Jumbo-pop for his son.
    The café owner refused to serve them, though.
He didn't like having foxes in his store.
    Judy knew that was wrong.

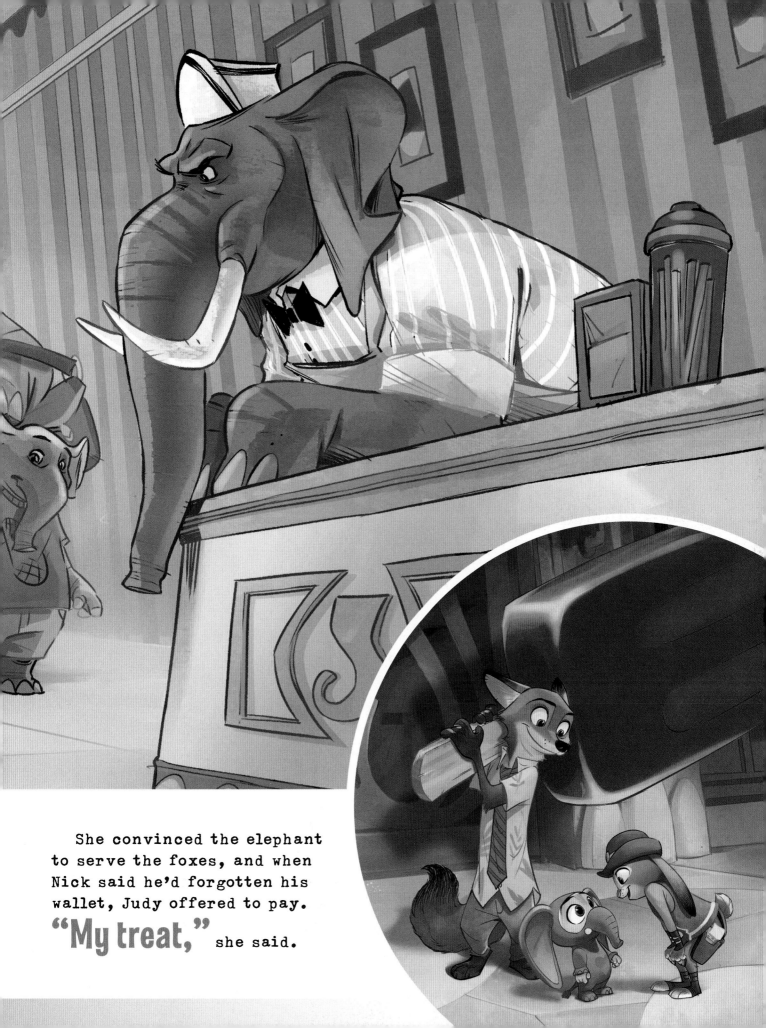

She convinced the elephant to serve the foxes, and when Nick said he'd forgotten his wallet, Judy offered to pay. **"My treat,"** she said.

Judy felt pleased with herself . . . until she spotted Nick and his son melting the Jumbo-pop and collecting the liquid into jugs. Then the two refroze it into new, little ice pops. Nick sold his "pawpsicles" to lemmings and made a huge profit.

To top it off, Nick's "son" turned out to be an adult fennec fox, with a very deep voice.

Judy had been tricked!

Judy confronted Nick. "You lied to me!"
"It's called a hustle, sweetheart," he replied. Nick believed that an animal could only be what it already was. He pointed to himself. **"Sly fox."**

Then he pointed to Judy. **"Dumb bunny."**
"I'm not a dumb bunny!"
"Right." Nick smirked. "And that's not wet cement."
Judy looked down and sighed. She had a lot to learn.

That evening, Judy felt discouraged as she took the subway to her apartment and made herself a carrot dinner for one.

She was glad when her mom and dad called, but within a few seconds, they noticed Judy's meter maid uniform.

"She's not a real cop," said her dad. **"Our prayers have been answered!"**

Judy squirmed. She knew she could succeed. She just needed a chance.

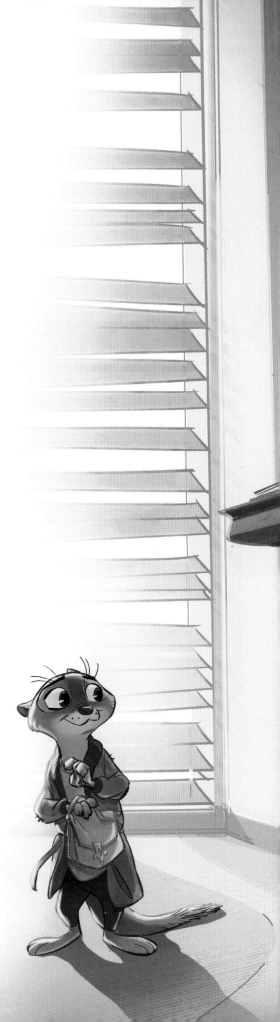

The next day, Judy got her chance. A weasel robbed a nearby flower shop! Judy chased the thief through Little Rodentia and captured the weasel by dropping a donut sign over his head.

Chief Bogo was furious. The chase had disrupted Little Rodentia, all because the thief had stolen what looked like moldy onions.

Just then, Mrs. Otterton entered. Her husband was missing and she needed help. "I'll find him," volunteered Judy.

Assistant Mayor Bellwether, a sheep, made sure Judy got the case.

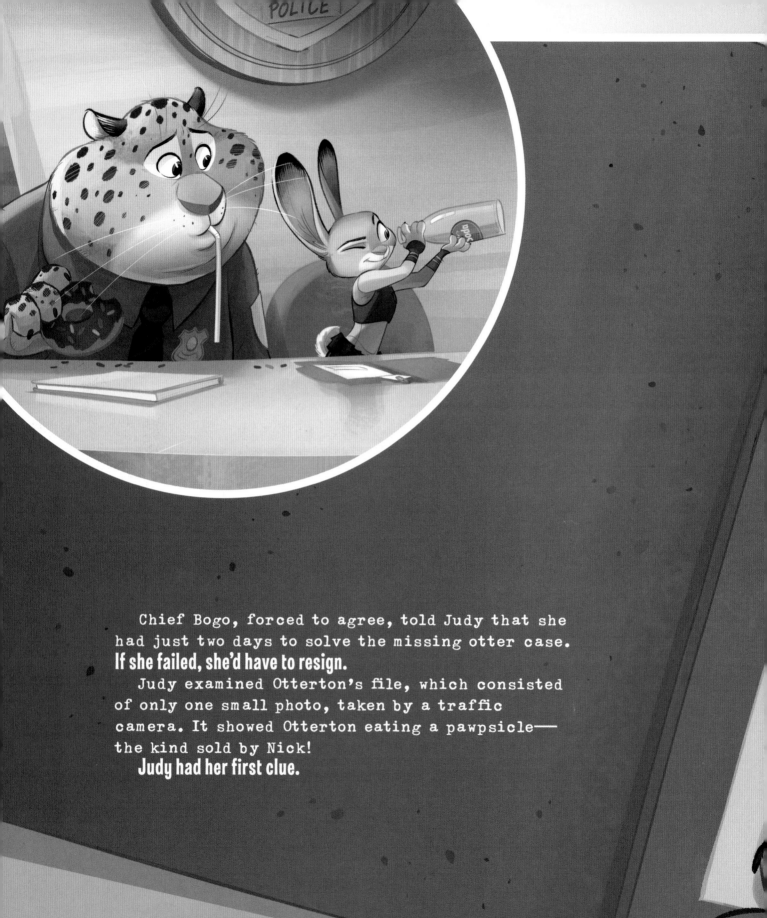

Chief Bogo, forced to agree, told Judy that she had just two days to solve the missing otter case. **If she failed, she'd have to resign.**

Judy examined Otterton's file, which consisted of only one small photo, taken by a traffic camera. It showed Otterton eating a pawpsicle— the kind sold by Nick!

Judy had her first clue.

Nick refused to help—until Judy secretly recorded the
fox bragging about his scams. Then she said she'd arrest
him if he didn't help.
   "It's called a hustle, sweetheart." Judy laughed.
   Forced to help, Nick found a witness who had seen
Otterton getting into a car. Nick said his friend Flash
at the DMV could look up the license plate number.

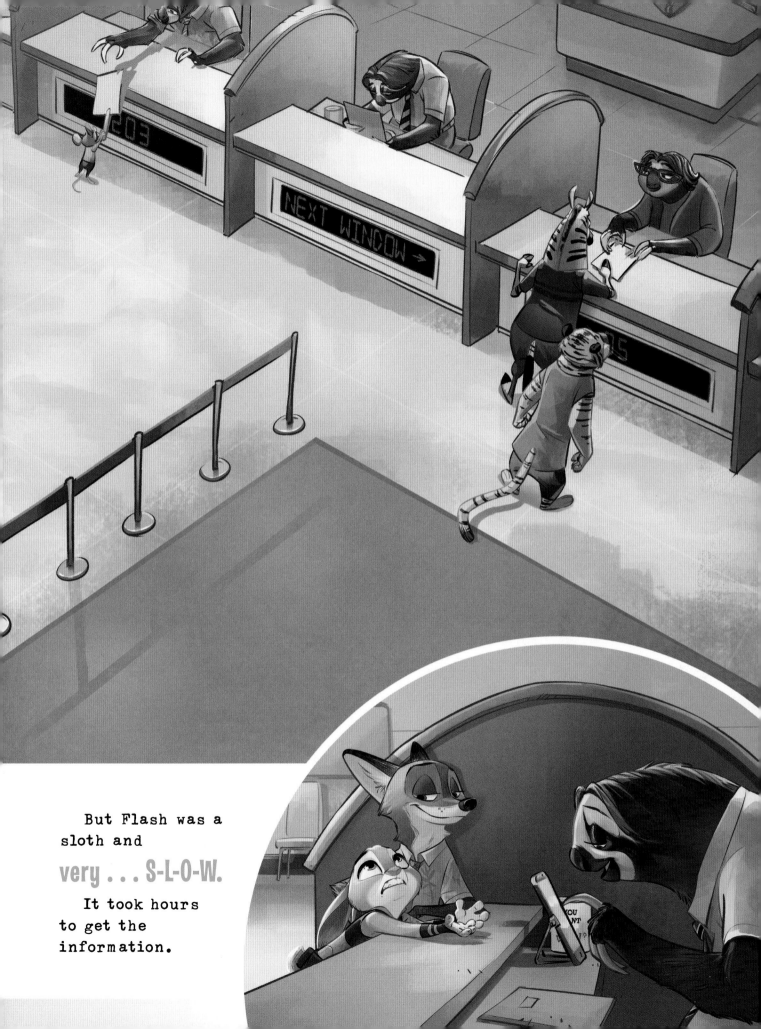

But Flash was a sloth and

very . . . S-L-O-W.

It took hours to get the information.

It turned out that the car belonged to Mr. Big, a notorious crime boss in Tundratown. But Mr. Big didn't like Nick, and he ordered his thugs to drop Nick and Judy into an ice pit.

"Wait!" shouted Mr. Big's daughter, Fru Fru. "That bunny saved my life!" Judy had saved Fru Fru during the weasel chase in Little Rodentia.

Mr. Big was grateful. "I sent the car for Otterton," he explained. "But he went crazy, scared my driver half to death, and disappeared."

Judy and Nick went to the Rainforest District to talk to Mr. Big's driver, Manchas. The nervous jaguar said that Otterton had yelled something about the night howlers just before turning into a savage beast.

Then **Manchas went savage, too!** Judy called for backup as
she and Nick ran for their lives.

They escaped when Judy managed to handcuff Manchas
to a tree.

Strangely, by the time the ZPD arrived, there was no trace of Manchas. Chief Bogo didn't believe a word of Judy's story and asked for her badge.

"No," said Nick. **"You gave her forty-eight hours. We still have ten left."**

As they departed, Judy thanked Nick for sticking up for her.

Just then, the fox had an idea. The traffic cameras would have recorded what happened to Manchas! But how could they get access to the videos?

"I've got a friend at city hall," said Judy.

When Nick and Judy arrived at city hall,
Assistant Mayor Bellwether was trying to get the
mayor's attention.

"Clear my afternoon," snapped Mayor
Lionheart. "I'm going out."

"But, sir!" cried Bellwether. The door slammed
in her face and sent her papers flying. "Oh, mutton
chops," she muttered.

Bellwether was happy to help Nick and Judy. She showed them the footage from the **traffic cameras.** The video showed wolves putting Manchas into a van!

"Night howlers!" Judy exclaimed. "That's what Manchas was afraid of . . . wolves!" She nodded. **"If they took Manchas, they probably took Otterton, too."**

The van drove onto a back road that led out of town. Nick had a good idea where it went.

Nick took Judy to the old Cliffside Asylum. A pack of wolves guarded the entrance. Judy started to howl.

"Ooooo! Ooooo!"

As she expected, the wolves joined in. They couldn't help it! "Ooooo! Ooooo!"

While the wolves howled, Judy and Nick snuck inside.

Judy and Nick found Manchas, Otterton, and the other missing mammals. They'd all gone savage!

Just then, Mayor Lionheart and a doctor walked in.
Judy quickly hid and used her phone to record their
conversation.

The doctor said he didn't know why the animals had gone
wild. "But we both know what they have in common," he added.

"We can't keep this a secret."

Lionheart was worried that the truth would make the
city panic.

Suddenly, **Judy's phone rang.** She and Nick had to make a
daring escape.

Judy took the video to Chief Bogo—she had cracked the case of the missing mammals! Mayor Lionheart was arrested and Assistant Mayor Bellwether took over.

Judy handed Nick a ZPD application. "I could really use a partner," she said. Nick grinned.

At a press conference, Judy admitted she didn't know why these animals had gone savage. She did note that all of them were predators.
"Could this happen again?" asked a reporter.
"Yes," said Judy. "It's possible."

After the press conference, Nick was angry.
Judy had made it sound like any predator could
go savage at any time!

"You think I might go nuts, too?"

he asked.

He tossed the ZPD application aside and
walked away.

All over Zootopia, prey animals became
distrustful of predators as even more of them
went savage.

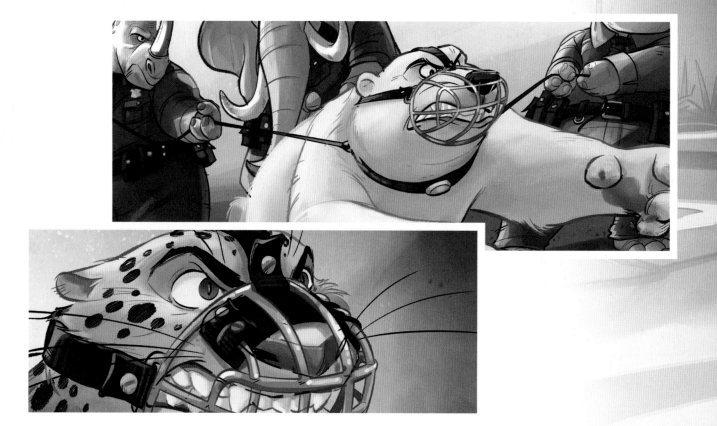

Saddened at having caused so much
trouble, Judy quit the ZPD.

Judy returned to Bunnyburrow. While working at her family's farm stand, Judy was startled to hear her dad warning kids to stay away from the night howlers, flowers that made animals go crazy.

"Night howlers are flowers, not wolves," Judy realized. "The flowers are making predators go savage. That's it!"

Judy dropped everything, jumped into the family pickup truck, and drove back to Zootopia.

Judy wanted Nick to help her find out who was making predators go crazy. But first she owed him an apology.

"I judged you and feared you," she said. "I really am a dumb bunny. Can you forgive me?"

Nick played back a recording:

"I really am a dumb bunny."

"Don't worry," he said. "You can erase it—in forty-eight hours."

Judy gave Nick a hug. They were partners again!

Judy and Nick started by questioning the weasel Judy had arrested. He admitted that he had been stealing night howler bulbs and selling them to a secret laboratory. The lab was in an old subway car. To get in, Judy and Nick had to sneak past the guards and shimmy through a window.

The lab was turning night howler flowers into a bright-blue serum. Judy sprang into action. She kicked the lab worker out and locked the doors.

"We have to get this evidence to the ZPD!"

Judy and Nick tried to escape in the subway car, but the guard rams climbed aboard. The train careened through the city. When it pulled into a station, the train derailed. Nick and Judy jumped off just as it exploded!

Judy couldn't believe it. They'd lost the evidence!

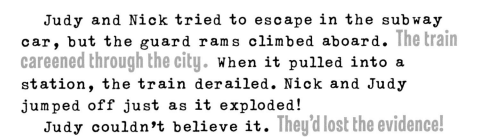

"Except for this," said Nick, holding up a case of serum.

Nick followed Judy into the Natural History Museum—a shortcut to the ZPD.

Inside the museum, Bellwether was waiting. "I'll go ahead and take that case," she said.

Judy gasped. Mayor Bellwether was behind the whole plot! Bellwether knew there were many more prey animals than predators. All she had to do was make prey afraid of predators— then the prey animals, with their greater numbers, could take over Zootopia. And Bellwether would be their leader!

Bellwether's thugs cornered Judy and Nick and grabbed the case. Then Bellwether shot Nick with a serum-filled dart!

The fox growled—he was going savage! Judy backed away.

"Your plan won't work," Judy bravely told Bellwether.

"Fear always works," she said. "And I'll dart a million more predators to prove it!"

Suddenly, Nick stopped growling. He and Judy had swapped the night howler serum with blueberries!

"From Hopps Family Farm," said Nick. **"They're delicious!"**

Bellwether was furious.

"I framed Lionheart. I can frame you, too!"

But Nick had recorded Bellwether's confession on Judy's carrot pen: *"And I'll dart a million more predators to prove it!"*

Judy smiled at Bellwether.

"It's called a hustle, sweetheart."

With the case closed and the missing mammals recovered, doctors quickly discovered a cure for those animals that had gone savage.

Nick became the first fox to join the ZPD, and Judy spoke at his graduation. She advised the new officers to look within themselves to try to make the world a better place.

"Change starts with all of us," she said.
Everyone cheered!